THE WAKING & MAKING
OF PAUL GAUGUIN

Books by Roy Holland

Insights and Outsights: Poems by Roy Holland
> Cape Town: David Philip. ISBN: 0864861214

Just A Bit Touched: Tales of Perspective
> Writers Club Press.   ISBN: 0-595-15874-9

Flakes of Dark and Light: Tales from Southern Africa and Elsewhere
> Writers Club Press.   ISBN: 0-595-17423-X

Pivot of Violence: Tales of the New South Africa
> Writers Club Press.   ISBN: 0-595-15821-8

News From Parched Mountain: Tales from the Karoo in the new South Africa
> Writers Club Press. ISBN: 0-595-14612-0

The Waking & Making of Paul Gauguin –
Conversations with Himself: A Play for Voices
> Diadem Books, 2008. ISBN: 978-0-9559741-3-7

Alan Paton Speaking: The Lintrose Conversations
> Edited by Charles Muller. Diadem Books, 2008.

The Jonathan Three (published by Diadem Books):

The Nowhere Man   ISBN: 978-0-9559741-0-6
Journey Towards Himself   ISBN: 978-0-9559741-1-3
Now Lead Me Home ISBN: 978-0-9559741-2-0

THE WAKING & MAKING OF
PAUL GAUGUIN

Conversations with Himself

A Play for Voices

by

Roy Holland

DB

DIADEM BOOKS

Published by Diadem Books

For information, please contact:

Diadem Books
Ocean Surf
CLASHNESSIE
IV27 4JF
Scotland UK

www.diadembooks.com

Front cover
Hybrid tree peony 'Gauguin' – Paeoniaceae hybrid

Cover design by Angus Muller

ISBN: 978-0-9559741-3-7

DRAMATIS PERSONAE

(Not in order of speaking)

Narrator

Paul Gauguin
The Five Inner Voices of the Five senses
Mette Gauguin

Clovis Gauguin
Ward Sister
Ward Nurse

Captain

Playing time – 60 minutes

Voices of Gauguin

The voices all belong to Gauguin, except the Narrator (and those specifically named, of course). As he comes to full consciousness after his illness, he comes slowly to a new self-awareness also, and of his mission of himself as an artist. This is what the play is about.

Voice One is the sense of Hearing, or the Ear; Voice Two is Smell, or the Nose; Voice Three is Touch, the Fingers; Voice Four is Taste, the Tongue; last of all is Voice Five, Sight or Eye, for him, the most important. Only when the former are alive can the last one function properly: then he is fully functioning as an artist. But it is at great cost to his physical and psychic health he has achieved this wholeness. They are represented in the order in which his senses fully return to him, when, only then, at last, is he able to realize fully his artistic mission.

Foreword

In 1883, when Gauguin was 35 years old, a family man and a successful stockbroker, he made a secret decision to become a painter – although he was a beginning amateur, who had had no recognition by that time. He hid this decision from everybody, including his wife. But, it was only in 1885 – after a disastrous quarrel with her in Copenhagen, where they were staying with the Gads, his wife's relations – he actually separated from her and his children. Then, he spent the best part of a miserable two years in Paris, where he painted, lived in poverty and was often ill. (For a short time in this period, he lived in Brittany, and first found himself as a painter.)

However, in search of the natural life, he decided to go to Tobago, where he thought the living was cheap. He never arrived there; he went first to Panama with Charles Laval. For a short while, they worked as navvies, digging the Panama Canal. It was so ghastly an experience that they ended up in Martinique, where Gauguin was struck down by a tropical fever and dysentery.

It was during this illness, in 1887, when Gauguin was 39 years old, that the battle I have imagined in his body, and in his mind, and in his moral nature, could have taken place.

Roy Holland

ix

THE WAKING & MAKING
OF PAUL GAUGUIN

(Fade in tropical noises at night. sound of breathing, someone fitfully asleep. A bed creaks. Sound of shoes over a wooden floor in a fairly large room, two people walking. Clink of basins, medical instruments. Footsteps stop. Other sounds continue.)

NURSE
(Suggestion of a French accent.)
He seems to be asleep, Sister. Shall I wake him?

SISTER
(Can be a French accent.)
No; just take his temperature.

NURSE
It's forty-one! His fever is growing, sister.

SISTER

Bring it down. He is breathing badly.

NURSE

With—?

SISTER:

Of course! What else?

NURSE

But it addles his wits.

SISTER:

It's the best we can do.

(Fade out the sounds of the hospital ward. Then fade them in again, slightly altered to indicate morning. The sound of curtain rings, in two staccato movements, going along a rod.)

NARRATOR

Morning!

(Gentle singing in the background.)

NARRATOR

The Creoles are singing their orisons. Oh, the ebonies of Martinique!

(Bring up the sound of the sea, fade, and keep behind the following dialogue. Perhaps fade out singing, or keep it there, according to director.)

NARRATOR

Saint Pierre, capital city of a tiny island, in the Lesser Antilles. The year is eighteen-eighty-seven.

Listen!

(Bring up the sound of the sea for a moment.)

NARRATOR

The Caribbean is building its corals, its intricate corals. Such colours! Such corals! The man, who is very sick, cannot see them. Cannot see the great volcano of Mont Pelee, the forests of mahogany and rosewood; cannot taste the spindrift in the breeze. Nor the salted baldness of the sea, blue as an eye, fingered by the yellow sands. Oh, how he yearns for the buckets and spades and castles of his blameless years! But, he is dead to the world, dodoed in his dreams. Watch! He is twitching. He moans. It troubles him – this malady, this swelter of heat. It is unselving him. He is unpeeling his rinds. He is random, like water

GAUGUIN

(Moaning gently)

NARRATOR

No tastes in his tongue, no touch on his fingers. Yet the bright flowers open. How they proliferate! The mangoes, the guavas, the lemons, the oranges, the corossols! But he is unravelling. The currents of his nerves drift, shapeless as vapour. He is urgeless. Still, the day must open.

(The sound of curtains opening is resumed. two or three times. a pause. a momentary distortion of sound to show that the following dialogue is occurring in the patient's head.)

VOICE ONE

It is time for you to awake. Rouse yourself, man! Wake up! The curtains are cawing like crows. Hear them?
(Pause) Answer me!

GAUGUIN

(An indeterminate response)

VOICE ONE

Are you there?

GAUGUIN

(Another attempt to respond)

VOICE ONE

Are you trying? Try. That's better!

GAUGUIN

(Another attempt, slight improvement)

VOICE ONE

Breathe! Answer me! Listen. Become!

GAUGUIN

(With great difficulty)
I c-can't.

VOICE ONE

You can! You can! The syllables will accumulate. Allow the words to germinate under your tongue. The slow lymphs! Let them sprout in your mouth

.

GAUGIN

(Attempting)

For—once— .

VOICE ONE

That's it! Easy now! The sentence will run. They will ramify. Think of the corals, the serums! Concurrences!

GAUGUIN

I'm trying.

VOICE ONE

Bravo! Now, answer me. Become!

GAUGUIN

(Voice becoming stronger).
What was the question?

VOICE ONE

That sounds normal enough.

(Another staccato burst of the curtains.)

VOICE ONE

The curtains are crowing again. Can't you hear them?

GAUGUIN

For once in my life, I seem—I seem—

VOICE ONE

What?

GAUGUIN

To have reached a circumlocution.

VOICE ONE

Hurrah! Now, remove it.

GAUGIN

How?

VOICE ONE

What do you hear? *Attention!*

(French being spoken in the background.)

(Then silence – except for the morning sounds of the hospital ward. A curtain twitches softly. The sea is still faintly in the background.)

GAUGUIN

Nothing. Absolutely nothing. Only you.

VOICE 1

Who?

GAUGUIN:

You! *(Pause)*.

By the way, who are you?

VOICE ONE

(Laughs).

I wondered when you'd ask.

GAUGUIN

Now, it's your turn.

VOICE ONE

(Laughs again).

Yes, I suppose it is. It's difficult for me to say.

GAUGUIN

Why?

VOICE ONE

Because you won't believe me.

GAUGUIN

Try me!

VOICE ONE

All right. Wait for it! I'm YOU!

GAUGUIN

What?

VOICE ONE

Or if you prefer, a part of you

.

GAUGUIN

: A part of me! Which part? I hear you out there? I'm here. You are
there!

VOICE ONE

: That's an illusion! I only seem to be out here.

GAUGUIN

Where are you, then?

VOICE ONE

Inside you. Wherever.

GAUGUIN:

What kind of an answer is that? Wherever is an adverb,
not an answer

.

VOICE ONE

Or a conjunction. Of you and me.

GAUGUIN

Oh, very clever! Prove it!

VOICE ONE

Right! Pay attention!

GAUGUIN

I'm all ears.

VOICE ONE

Touché! Felicitous, indeed! Go on! Feel your ears! *(Pause)* Feel them!

GAUGUIN

(Pause). I c-can't!

VOICE ONE

Why not?

GAUGUIN

I can't move.

VOICE ONE

: Exactly! You're a captive

GAUGUIN

You mean, a prisoner?

VOICE ONE

Non! Well, in a manner of speaking, Yes!

NARRATOR

A prisoner of his infirmity, made captive by his illness. Myriads of cells are in commotion: Moving, fusing, dissolving, losing identity. He becomes a randomness, a nullity. A nobody.

VOICE ONE

Except for me. I'm throwing you a lifeline. Listen!

(Bring in the sound of ticking.)

VOICE ONE

The ward is full of clocks. All of them are ticking. Carafes and clocks. Every patient watered and timed.

(Increase the ticking with clinking of glasses.)

VOICE ONE

Can you hear them?

(Pause)

GAUGUIN

No! Nothing but a mode of silence. And a medley of egg-timers. I'm deafened by the sound. Their sands are drifting, their waters pouring.

VOICE ONE

Ironies are wasted on me! Where are you islanded?

GAUGUIN

You're the know-all, the clever-dick, the one with the answers!

VOICE ONE

In your hospital bed, Saint Pierre, Lesser Antilles.

GAUGUIN

The Caribbean, The World, The Universe. That's a kid's game!

VOICE ONE

You've forgotten The Galaxy, and The Cosmos.

GAUGUIN

I'm not well, you know.

VOICE ONE

But improving—which brings me back to our topic. You! What you think of as you is only a tint in the spectrum, a flicker of phosphorous on the vanishing wave, a faltering candle in an empty house.

GAUGUIN ONE

In which you are also confined, remember.

VOICE ONE

But only as a scout, an outrider. I bring messages back to Headquarters.

GAUGUIN

At dawn!

VOICE ONE

For the moment.

GAUGUIN

Exactly – who are you?

VOICE ONE

Haven't you guessed?

GAUGUIN

No.

VOICE ONE

A member of your holy five, that elected handful which brings innumerableness to one.

GAUGUIN

How grand! By that, I suppose you to mean the first of your group to recover?

VOICE ONE

You've got it!

GAUGUIN

. Let me guess.

.

VOICE ONE

I know that you know.

GAUGUIN

So – How come, no clocks?

VOICE ONE

Wait a little! Be patient!

GAUGUIN

That is what I am – a patient.

VOICE ONE

You're winning. Listen to yourself being wilful. That's progress!
Remember? You couldn't reply, at first

.

GAUGUIN

I know. Our Man from Nirvana. The Gone-Between from Ignorance to
Nothingness

.

VOICE ONE

Oh, very good! Go on! Go on!

GAUGUIN

Go on! Go on!… You sound like a parrot. You are the one who's
shirking. If you were competent, I'd be hearing the clocks.

VOICE ONE

On the contrary, you would converse, and use my talents, not question
and demand.

13

GAUGUIN

Queries are in my blood. My corpuscles are pale with questions, and you prevaricate. You say it is me. But it isn't me speaking. I am a stranger to myself. My tongue is a sundered hulk in the dock of my mouth. It is mouldering away.

VOICE ONE

Forget your tongue! Like the sea, it overflows with vocables and sadness. But your ears! Are you receiving me? Or have the depredations of the fever rendered you deaf?

GAUGUIN

A few crackles here and there, and a tingling in my nose. Otherwise, you're too loud and too clear!

VOICE ONE

Good!

(A breaker crashes suddenly onto rocks.)

GAUGUIN

What was that?

VOICE ONE

You heard it? Well done! We're reviving your *esprit de corps*!

(The sea gets choppier and fussier.)

VOICE ONE

Listen to its agitation! Its gabble and hiss! The anger and slash of its comings—

GAUGUIN

—And goings? A time ago, according to you, it was full of the sounds of sadness. What changed?

VOICE ONE

So you heard it?

GAUGUIN

I heard it.

VOICE ONE

The clocks! What about the clocks?

GAUGUIN

Tick-tock! Tick-tock! Ceaseless as microbes, extending dimensions.

VOICE ONE

Another of your circumlocutions, I suppose? Now, you really are on the way to recovery.

GAUGUIN

That aroma! Delicious!

VOICE TWO

A galore of fruits and summer scents—

NARRATOR

Says his second sense—

GAUGUIN

Who spoke?

NARRATOR:

A mixer of memories and dreams. His world is now a place of odours, as well as of sounds. His desires infuse, blending their perfumes in his brain. A flicker in his consciousness engrosses itself. He is becoming. Like a crystal, he is growing. He will rise, by and by, into brightness, into morning.

GAUGUIN

Guava, ripe guava! How could I ever forget?

VOICE TWO

And the scents of Lima? Your childhood in Peru? The smell of bamboo? Your nursemaid's sweat? And the tamarind?

GAUGUIN

Them too! But the freshness of guava! Especially that! No sooner had I docked in Martinique, than a girl, sixteen no more – yet lissom and full as a woman – offered herself to me. She had opened and split the guavas, fresh from the trees, and pressed them against the nipples of her breasts, and held them out to me. The elixirs of St Pierre! How they would bind me to her, betrothed for ever, if I had accepted them! Oh, the angst of guavas! The ardours of sable! The perfumes and mores of Martinique!

VOICE TWO

And the *arondissements* of Paris, Rouen and Brittany?

GAUGUIN

Pont-Aven, Toulon, and old Bordeaux. Commotions of wines and garlic! Exhalations of coffee, freshly ground! And the cheeses, ripe with summer milk, and their salads, garnished with camomile and fennel! I remember!

VOICE ONE

Do you remember the noises they made?

VOICE TWO

Attention! You've had your chance. Your auditing must wait.

GAUGUIN:

Noises? Noises? I only sense the sounds of growth. The rest is odours!

VOICE TWO

: That's right! Assemble them!

GAUGUIN

Childhood in Peru! The ships were full of spices, and their holds of aromatic darkness, and their sails of salt. In Lima, till I was seven, I spoke Spanish. I learned French later in Paris. With difficulty.

VOICE TWO

Remember the smell of pimentos, and the tola shrubs?

GAUGUIN

That tropical savour! That animal smell! It lingers! Ah, the nose! I slept as a child with my sister and the maid, who lay as naked as an egg. It hurts!

VOICE TWO

If you're hurting, you're alive! And the walnut leaves you crushed and used as snuff?

GAUGUIN

That's right! I remember! My palms were redolent with their juice and oils.

(Bring in the sounds of branches creaking gently in a breeze)

.

GAUGUIN

And I lay for days beneath its branches, waiting for its nuts to fall. But they did not fall. My mother found me first.

VOICE TWO

Asleep! *(interjected)*

.

(Superimpose voice from the past over the sound of branches creaking.)

MOTHER:

Paul! Paul! Where are you, Paul?

GAUGUIN

Asleep, Maman! *(Boy's voice)*

(Make transition back to the dialogue. Fade out branches creaking.)

GAUGUIN

I want to sleep, again.

VOICE ONE

And I had such high hopes for you!

VOICE TWO

St Pierre is full of scents. There are perfumes enough to smell for ever.

GAUGUIN

I am tired. My dreams are mortal. They're building spontaneous temples for me to kneel in. They wish to shape me for transparency, to walk in the sun and cast no shadow: We Borgias have a stoical ash.

NARRATOR

He is fading again. He is falling. The archer's shaft curves to the earth at the end of its flight..

GAUGUIN

The world is falling towards me.

NARRATOR

You are falling like a walnut, like an arrow.

GAUGUIN

To a smallness! The world is falling towards the walnut. It falls towards the apple, as Newton knew. To me.

VOICE ONE

Think of Emile, your eldest son! What did he say?

GAUGUIN

Who?

VOICE ONE

About the toast! What did he say?

GAUGUIN

Toast?… Oh, yes! Now, I recall. Emile said: 'Eating toast is the noise that wolves make, eating people.'

VOICE ONE

Bravo! Bravo! Now, Schuffenecker! Your friend! You named your son after him.

GAUGUIN

I did, I did! Schuff, old Schuff!

(Bring in the sound of feet shuffling.)

GAUGUIN

Schuff-Schuff! His soul is a pair of slippers, a shuffle of leaves, a shuffle of leavings. How to classify him? I never could. Two conflicting lives. A negative neuro-muscular Type A, and.a member of the *petit bourgeoisie* who paints! A Parisian gentleman with a forbidden passion! Schuff, oh Schuff! Where are you falling?

VOICE TWO

(Urgently) Think of the odour of grapefruit, the winds of the Auvergne?

GAUGUIN

(Gives a groan)

VOICE THREE

It's my turn now! Cool as an eyelid, I am, and mild as calamine.

NARRATOR

A new voice, a new sense. The third of his holy five. They are
desperate to survive and to nudge him back to knowingness.

*(Bring in the sound of a breeze through the open windows and the sea
rolling onto the shore and the rocks. Keep gently in the background
for a moment, then fade.)*

VOICE THREE

The silks of St Pierre! They stroke your cheeks, like the dark hair of
your mother, Aline-Marie. Feel them! Move the back of your hand
along its shores. Feel the swathes your fingers make in the sand: those
ruts are your little roads to recollection.

(Bring in the branches and leaves & the sound of whittling.)

VOICE THREE

That time under the walnut tree, when you carved the handle for your
dagger, are the chips and whittlings of memory. Remember! And your
mother's room, in Lima! Remember!

NARRATOR

But he does not stir.

VOICE ONE

It's no good. He's deaf!

VOICE TWO

But he has a nose, a conk, a schnozzle, a hooter! And Martinique has odours! The air itself is made of spices and souvenirs. He's got the nose of a Borgia. It can hook itself to effluvia by its shape alone! The blood of the Borgias, and of Peruvian Indians, slides through his veins. His sense of smell is positively ancestral. Wake up! Breathe! Inhale! Sniff!

VOICE ONE

If he cannot hear, he cannot respond, nose or not!

VOICE THREE

And his fingers are touchless. They are falling like Autumn leaves, from the branches of his nerves

.

(Fade up the sound of the clocks in the ward and the clink of glasses, the creak of bed springs, et cetera.)

NARRATOR

Light fades. Time passes. He has suffered a setback. They multiply – the microbes. They teem – the bacteria. They dilate and close: the pupils of mad eyes. Time passes. He has cooled. It is medicine time.

(Bring in the sounds of the nurses moving about, as before. a snatch of Creole singing in the background.)

SISTER

He is sleeping calmly now, Nurse. Moisten his lips. Change his sheets, and gown. Administer his anodyne.

.

NARRATOR

He is bringing together the cellular life of his mind. Those coralled shoals! Yet, he is drowned. Sensations are deep and indiscriminate. He must pierce their surface, find a point on which to stand, to breathe, to see, to come to consciousness again.

(There is a sound of drinking and swallowing.)

NURSE

C'est ca, mon ami, c'est ca. Drink up!

VOICE FOUR

The taste of dereliction! The Bols and Bitters of pharmacopoeia! The astringencies of pick-me-ups!

NARRATOR

Says his palate. Flavours defoliate. Their buds are closing up. They are stunned. They are falling. They are still.

NURSE

Dormez bien, mon pauvre.

NARRATOR

Says the nurse, insouciant as an aperitif.

.

(Footsteps walk away from the bed, down the ward. Silence.)

NARRATOR

And he, no longer focussed by the self-regarding opiate of pain, is empty and silent, too. Time passes. The sun is pouring its wines into the sea. Tree-crickets shuffle their wings like cardsharps in the evening shebeens. The moon enlightens its sinless self like a wafer of bright shewbread; and the exuberances of Martinique release themselves: The laughter of negresses in their brilliant wraps; the singing of children; the glistening of their blacknesses, the rattling of banana leaves; the breezes from the reefs; the quarrelling of Chinamen and Indians. And while the darkness fumes, holding fecundity in its breath, the scentless hibiscus deepens its hues. Slowly, slowly, his fever abates. His senses revive. Gathering to a fullness, memory is filling its honeycombs, and his dreams are buzzing like bees.

(Sounds of a ship under sail mix with those of the hospital ward at the start of a new day. Fade out ship sounds.)

NARRATOR

It is morning.

GAUGUIN

Where am I?

VOICE FIVE

Our galaxy. It is I!

NARRATOR

Says a new voice. Says his seeing sense.

GAUGUIN

'I'? Who is 'I'? A faceless pronoun! What do you mean? Our galaxy?

VOICE FIVE

It is eighty thousand light-years wide. A light-year equals six million million miles. The light of the sun takes eight minutes to reach us. Open your eyes, and blink!

GAUGUIN

Mon Dieu! Another of them to plague me!

VOICE FIVE

It is falling across your face. Look!

GAUGUIN

Warm on my lids and blind on my lashes. I cannot see; but if it's any satisfaction to you, there's a sense of glory in my eyes.

VOICE FIVE

That will certainly do! How come?

GAUGUIN

I had a dream.

(Fade in the sound of a guitar, children singing in the background, domestic sounds.)

VOICE FIVE

A dream?

GAUGUIN

A mixture of nightmare and vision. I was back with Mette and the children. We'd left Rouen for Denmark; I had given up my job on the Bourse, with old Bertin. I had started to paint. We stayed with the Gads, Mette's parents and relatives in Copenhagen. They abused me. (I was well on the way to beggary.) Mette nagged and nagged. It was money, and the neighbours. And money! The home, and money. Mette is a philistine. The Gadds are as tight as predikants: a mixture of arrogance, and ignorance, and authority. Her sister's a witch, casting icy spells. We fought!

(Discord on a guitar.)

GAUGUIN

Oh, how wicked the passion that parted us!

(Another guitar chord to signal a flashback.)

METTE

You are selfish and thoughtless and cruel! They call you a ne'er-do-well. You want to be idle and dissolute. What about me? What about the children? What about us?

GAUGUIN

I will send you money from Paris. I hate the Danes. I hate Denmark. I hate the climate.

METTE

We cannot live on air and promises. My folks are—!

GAUGUIN

—dammers-up and destroyers! – Oh, Mette, prevent them! Prevent them!… Ash tree, ash tree, Yggdrasil, tree of the world, protect me from their spells, their witchcraft! If I do not dare everything, I dare nothing. Nothing!

METTE

At whose expense? You dump on them a wife, and five children. You fiddle about with clay and paint, and sponge on them relentlessly, and call yourself—

GAUGUIN

Dare everything, or I dare nothing.

METTE

Go, then! Go! Go!

(A small silence. then a few guitar sounds. A short interval of ship and sea sounds. Fade. Re-establish hospital sounds.)

GAUGUIN

I went. It was a turning-point. There was no going back. I took little Clovis, my six-year old son, back to Paris with me. I wanted all the children. But it was impossible. It tore me to bits to leave them there in the North. But Paris, the winter of '85 Clovis was ill. The poor little mite! *Mon pauvre!* My sister Marie agreed to look after him.

VOICE FIVE

What did you do?

GAUGUIN

I painted. I painted! The winters of eighty-five and eighty-six, I was driven like a madman. In the May of eighty-six, Pissaro set up the final exhibition for our group. They called us `Impressionistes'... I exhibited several works in wood, in marble, and nineteen canvasses. That year, I earned just two hundred and fifty francs!

VOICE FIVE

Are you describing the vision or the nightmare?

GAUGUIN

A sense of seeing, and a sense of humour, go together, I suppose?

VOICE FIVE

What happened then?

GAUGUIN

Pont-Aven happened. My hiding place in Brittany. My sanctum: Pension Marie-Jeanne Gloanec. One painting per month for board and lodging. A bargain – for her! But she was good to me. I would have starved that winter, if it hadn't been for her. I had a coterie, a school. I was king of the court! Charles Laval was there, Granchi, Dupuygodeau; and Schuff-Schuff sent Bernard. But I left.

VOICE FIVE

Why?

GAUGUIN

I was selling nothing. I returned to Paris, and rented a hovel on borrowed cash. My fame was growing. Every day it grew, but often I went three days together without a bite. I lost my health and strength. Eventually, I had to let Mette have Clovis back. *Mon pauvre*! We met at Saint Nazaire, to say goodbye.

(Discord on guitar. Wind and sea sounds. Dockside departure sounds. Hold in Background.)

METTE

There's nothing to say, except goodbye.

CLOVIS

Papa! Papa! Write to me! Write!

METTE

Goodbye, Paul.

VOICE FIVE

And what did you have to say?

GAUGUIN

Nothing! There was nothing I could say. The red leaves of my heart were full and falling. I did not know how to tell them that. I held my son so tight against me, he cried.

CLOVIS
Au revoir, Papa, au revoir!

(Fade out background sounds.)

VOICE FIVE
So then what did you do?

GAUGUIN
I left.

VOICE FIVE
Left?

GAUGUIN
By boat. From Saint Nazaire for Panama

VOICE FIVE
Panama?

GAUGUIN
That's right! Panama! My sister's husband owns a business, there. He offered me a job – in his store.

VOICE 5:
There's nothing there! Jungle! The Canal!

GAUGUIN

The canal spoiled all the pickings. We ended up, Charles Laval and I,
digging the blasted thing! Dysentery, mud, heat and flies, a few francs
a day. No French whores and no French wines. *Merde!* What a
sentence!

VOICE FIVE

And Charles Laval? What happened to him?

GAUGUIN:

Went home – to Paris.

VOICE FIVE

No wonder you said it was the nightmare.

GAUGUIN

A waking nightmare. As Saint Nazaire faded with distance, I slept and
dreamed, dreamed and slept.

(Gently behind dialogue, the sounds of a sailing ship at sea.)

VOICE FIVE

Is this the vision, now? The vision?

GAUGUIN

I floated above the earth. Somewhere! I don't know where. A vantage
point, a point of seeing. And I saw God, dazzlingly bright, reach down;
with His index finger, long and burning and alight. He touched the
mountains of the Auvergne into a spine of fire. Then, his finger
moved; to South America, Madagascar, Africa, the Antipodes, the
Marquesas, Tahiti and Martinique – the chosen lands of the earth! And

with the flame, the Holy Fire leaping from His fingers, He urged into the earth its beauties and its colours, until there blazed on the breast of the world a cross of unimaginable loveliness. I had seen! I was privileged to see them kindled there.... And that is when I knew.

VOICE FIVE

Knew what?

GAUGUIN

That I had to make the eyes of people everywhere see what He had quickened there. For seeing is a gift, a holy, holy thing. And He has granted it to me. So how can I deny it, no matter what?

(Fade out the sea and ship sounds.)

VOICE 5

And that is your vision?

GAUGUIN

Some of it!

VOICE FIVE

What is the rest of it?

GAUGUIN

That will have to wait—

VOICE FIVE

Till when?

GAUGUIN

Until I feel like telling you.

VOICE FIVE

So – at last you could see. And now?

GAUGUIN

Now?

VOICE FIVE

Here and now!

GAUGUIN

I don't know!

VOICE FIVE

Open them!

GAUGUIN FIVE

I will. But, first, there is another thing, another stream from the past I must dam up. Or it'll leak away like blood from a wound, de-naturing me:... Saint Nazaire, the last I saw of Mette and my son. I remember the day and the pain, the acrid odours of the chemical works, the wind off the sea, blowing the fumes inland, and inwards. The estuary of the Loire, widening, glittering, flat, full of air and space; and two solitary and single swans, riding apart, at peace, like visitations from a Northern world. They moved me deeply. I don't know why. I turned to look at the sea. Saint Nazaire, behind and at my back, blindly rode at anchor – full of the bourgeoisie, full of roly-poly mothers, the pockets of their aprons bursting with mothballs; and the fathers I couldn't belong to, their pockets bursting with francs. And was it nearly at Nantes, upriver, the railway lines ran straight into the Loire? There, the stinking English cutters stuck to the wharf, flying the colours of shirts and sea-boots and socks, and smelling abominably of bacon. The smelting works letting out its steam, and its thousands of calories of heat into the black waters of the Loire, encouraging the small black eels to breed. I'm recalling the pain of it!... I remember how Mette had gone, *mon petit chou*, the only woman I have ever loved. And my quintet of children, gone, too!

(A pause, then the daily sounds of the hospital ward reassert themselves, with suggestions of the sea behind them.)

VOICE FIVE

Ready now – to open them and look?

GAUGUIN

(Sighing) I suppose so!

VOICE FIVE

Well, go on! What do you see?

GAUGUIN

Nothing. Spaces. Only spaces.

VOICE FIVE

No colours? No light?

GAUGUIN

I'm skeleton-eyed. I see bones. The white peeled bones of a body of light.

VOICE FIVE

The window! Look at the window!... Now, what do you see?

(Slightly, the sounds of the sea.)

GAUGUIN

A bruise.

VOICE FIVE

You're hallucinating!

GAUGUIN

No! It is growing. Larger and darker, the bruise of the sea. A contusion. The colours remind me of Mette.

VOICE FIVE

It's your mind and your hurt that are looking.

GAUGUIN

Perhaps, perhaps. I am tired of looking.

VOICE FIVE

I think you'd better sleep. Your lids are closing. They're heavy with fevers and dreams. Rest, now. Rest.

GAUGUIN

Yes! Yes.

*(Fade out the suggestions of the sea. Keep hospital
sounds softly in background)*

NARRATOR

He sinks back into his pillows, sighing. And back into a furnace of
delirium, fusing again the clinker of his pain and the iron of himself to
a molten brew of sickness and unknowingness. What structures will
emerge? Will he cohere? Will he cool to a wholeness? Sane? One self?
Or become particled and desiccated? One must wait. Night must
breathe itself to dawn. And the scales of the beetles dry in the sun.
Perhaps when he wakes, the fever will have gone

.

(Bring up hospital sounds as at first, when play opened.)

NURSE

Sister, he feels cooler! The fever has calmed itself.

SISTER

Calmed, but not gone. Come! His pulse is still distressed. Sponge him
with rosewater.

(Footsteps going away. appropriate sounds of sponging, et cetera.)

NURSE

(Calling urgently) Sister! He is stirring. He is trying to sit up!

SISTER

Help him, help him! Gently!

NURSE

There! There!

GAUGUIN

Where am I? Who are you?

SISTER

Ah, bonjour, Monsieur! You have brought yourself back to us, eh?
Tres bien, Monsieur! We are glad to welcome you.

GAUGUIN

Where?

SISTER

A month of malaise has threshed and fretted you. Look at yourself! A
lath from the ceiling. Thin as hospital gruel. *Comment allez-vous,
monsieur*?

GAUGUIN

Not sure! I am dimmed. My spirits are quenched. I feel desiccated, like
cocoanut. I am thirsty.

SISTER

Give him water to drink, Nurse! We will return in an hour. Rest, now.
Later, you will eat; then, you'll feel better. *Allons! Allons!*

GAUGUIN

Attendez! Attendez!

SISTER

We have work to do, patients to see. Come, Nurse! *Venez!*

NARRATOR

A darkness is in his blood, and twilight fills his head. His senses hang apart, like drowsing bats waiting to awake. In time, they will stir, and begin their foraging. Even now, his fingers twitch along the sheets, opening themselves like mouths, hungry for sustenance. Memories stir like birds in the shadows of his mind, raucous as vultures. Let us move in closer to them

.

(The sounds of sailors at sea and sounds of franco-prussian battles.)

NARRATOR

Creak of rigging, clamour of water, sea-shanties, tar, the battles' hullabaloo, men o' War of Prussia and France. He's twenty-three again; at sea since he was seventeen.

*(Fade extraneous sounds. keep gentle ship sounds behind dialogue.
Bring in medley of voices out of the past.)*

VOICE ONE

Remember the weevils in the tack?

VOICE TWO

The water that tasted like slops?

VOICE THREE

The blisters!

VOICE FOUR

The smell of bilgewater and tar!

VOICE FIVE

A pipeful of good black shag?

CAPTAIN

The girls you scuttled in St Denis?

GAUGUIN

Aye, aye sir! Antoinette, Jeanne-Marie, Clothilde. Wakey-wakey!
Show a leg! I remember them all, Cap'n.

CAPTAIN

Do you remember your ship, the Jerome Napoleon?

GAUGUIN

Aye, aye sir! I do!

CAPTAIN

You Borgia! Tied to the deck of a ship of the line?

(Fade out ship sounds. Back in the ward.)

GAUGUIN

Aye, aye sir!

NARRATOR

Then, in Europe, the war ends. Remember that? Your return to the Bourse?

GAUGUIN

Of course, of course! Maman had died while I was at sea.

NARRATOR

So – Aline-Marie, *ta mere*, took her Peruvian loveliness into the waters of the dark. Her last thoughts were for you. She asked her mother's friend, Gustave Arosa, to find you a comfortable berth in Paris. He kept his word.

GAUGUIN

Yes. Arosa, rich as the Ali Khan, one of the gnomes of Paris: fixer, banker, *eminence grise*, collector of *Louis d'or and objets d'art*. He unlocked the door of the Bourse. His son-in-law, *directoir, Ferme de Bertin, rue Lafitte, Cite de Paris*, opened it wider and asked me in. I had a flair.

(Stock exchange sounds.)

GAUGUIN

At twenty-four, affluent, admired, I dressed like a great grandee.

(Fade out stock exchange sounds.)

GAUGUIN

But—inside, a salamander grew. A thing of fire that would not let me be. I burned. My dreams consumed me. I was damned.

NARRATOR

Then Mette appeared.

GAUGUIN

Ah, Mette! Her beauty was such, it doused my fires. I longed for domesticity. I wanted her; her elegance; her children; her home. I pledged my troth and ignored the heaps of ash that cooled inside me. Why didn't I know? What didn't I know? She said `Yes! Yes, I will. Yes!' But her eyes were cold and calculating, even then. There was I, handsome, a respectable job, money enough. The Strong Provider! I would do! I would do!

NARRATOR

And you married her.

(Snatch of bells, of preacher.)

GAUGUIN

Lutheran. Nordic. Precise. I married her. Not once. But twice. Twice! The second, a civil ceremony. The first, for her. The second for me. The first, cold. The second, warm. Warm! But it was no good!

NARRATOR

You loved her?

GAUGUIN

I loved her. I have never loved another woman the way I love Mette. But how to know?

NARRATOR

Know what?

GAUGUIN

That she's a philistine. That she will never let me close. That she will
never even ask to what her loyalty belongs: To money or to truth. It
wasn't me she wanted. It was what I represented, what she thought I
stood for: Security, status, a father for her bairns, a husband for the
neighbours to observe, —to see about. She used our marriage, the
entire twelve years of it, to raise—

(Pause)

NARRATOR

Your children?

GAUGUIN

No! Indifference—To a high art.

NARRATOR

Still feverish?

GAUGUIN

Perhaps. But my memories are cool. They congeal. They crack. There
is pain in the cast of them.

NARRATOR

They are also incomplete. You sing a solo! But it was a long duet.
What of her mezzo-soprano?

GAUGUIN

Have you got a taste for discord?… But Mette you shall have. I can
summon her: ask her. I'll bring her piety, her Nordic heart, her nay-
saying, her cadences of ice. Mette! Mette! Can you hear me? I have

called before, many times. But when she comes, she comes to collect. To count and collect. Mette! Mette!

METTE

Yes, I am here. What do you want?

GAUGUIN

Ask him! He is the prompter. I shall just spectate, and play the guitar for the children to sing.

(Background sounds of a guitar being struck & played gently to a voice singing a song. Sounds of delighted children, then their singing.)

CHILDREN SINGING
When, O when does Boney go to sea?
P'raps he'll sail in August, p'raps he'll stay `chez lui'

(Laughter of children.)

CHILD

Papa! Sing the other one.

ALL

Yes! Yes!

(Change of tune on the guitar.)

FATHER.

(Sings)

Napoleon was a general,
He had ten thousand men,
He marched them up to the top of the hill,
And he marched them down again.

*(Childish delight. Fade down guitar music, but continue in
background. Hold guitar behind narrator's word, too.)*

METTE

(Calling in the distance)

. Paul! Paul!

NARRATOR

But he feints and his footwork is good. He does not wish to confront
it—, his wholeness and truth, what he knows he will have to face. He
feels neutered. Because he is an artist he has a dedicated soul.
But because he is a man he is damned. His *métier* respects nothing.
Neither his personal nor private life. Neither his passion for family,
nor for his wife. His pledges as father, as spouse, though full of
compassion and love, have vowed to vanquish his pledges of
dedication and discipline – unto annihilation.

So, he cannot forget her, this wife from the North, this Mette. Nor
Emile, Clovis, Aline, Jean and little Paul.
Nor can he forget the judgment of Edouard Manet: "It isn't enough to
know your *metier*; it is necessary to be driven by it. No-one is a
painter, unless he loves painting more than he loves anything else."
But not a hint, not a word, not a whisper of his anguish will he convey
to his wife, who has no belief in his gift. And what her husband really
thinks she can never unearth.

(Fade up wife's voice calling.)

METTE

Paul! Paul!

(Discord struck loudly on the guitar. Then silence.)

GAUGUIN

(Wearily)

What now? I am given no peace. None!

METTE

She must go!

GAUGUIN

Who?

METTE

That Justine! That whore!

GAUGUIN

The housemaid? Justine – the housemaid?

METTE

Who else?

GAUGUIN

Mon dieu! What has she done?

METTE

What hasn't she done, that's what I want to know? And you can tell me.

GAUGUIN

I? How do I know what she's done?

METTE

Because you did it with her! I found this daub. Look at it!

GAUGUIN

My canvas! Mon '*Etude du Nu*'! It's a masterpiece.

METTE

It's an insult! To me! It's an indictment of you! The woman is naked!

GAUGUIN

Of course! It's a nude!

METTE

My own maid! In my own house!

GAUGUIN

Why not? She's posed before. For Manet, Renoir, Edgar Degas.

METTE

But her! Her!

GAUGUIN

You denied me the right to a model of my own. You refused them entry to your house. What else could I do? She's here! She's free! I took my chance.

METTE

Formidable! You took it! What else did you take?

GAUGUIN

I took what she willingly gave. Her nudity.

METTE

And what of herself? Her? Did you take her?

GAUGIN

Why don't you ask her yourself?

METTE

That's exactly what I'll do. And more! She'll be fired! The slut! Tomorrow! Your behaviour to me is incomprehensible. It's monstrous! Brutally selfish. You never think beyond your own well-being. That's all that matters! What of the children?

GAUGIN

You'll never understand! Your duty! My duty! Your unrelenting conscience. You'll never be a wife, my woman, *mon amoureuse.* You're only a mother. Look at the marriage of the Jobbe-Duvals! Poor as Job, wretchedly poor! But wretched they are not. They rise, they fly! Over their misery! Upwards! And why? They have unity of heart.

That's why! What have we got? Our gear! Our respectability! Your philistinism! – Ah, for me, it typifies the world! Don't be surprised! One day, I might seek for a wife who knows how to be a woman as well. *Une amante!*

METTE

You are a beguiler, a libertine, a betrayer of vows! That is the truth of things. Your art cannot alter that. Your precious Justine must go. Tomorrow—pouf! A bad memory!

GAUGUIN

You! You walk with your nose in the air, quite unaware it is stuffed up with false humility. Sin! Only one for your kind with a conscience like crystal! And your sense of duty that you put on like a suit of steel: Adultery! Sex! That is all. Nothing else is sin!

METTE

Sex is for marriage, which sanctifies and purifies it.

GAUGUIN

You want it confined and tamed like a pussy-cat. But it isn't tame. It is wild and untrammelled. If you want the essence of Elysium, and not the elixir of Monkey Hill, you must believe in the innocence of sensuality and become *en sauvage!*

METTE

What of decorum? What of self-restraint?

GAUGUIN

In your case, it all adds up to CON-straint, to abstention, to icy Nordic rituals!

METTE

A Nordic Monkey Hill! So that's what you think of our marriage, is it?

GAUGUIN

No, I don't! But you provoke me. You point at me. You call me
adulterer. You misconstrue me, misjudge me. That portrait, for
instance. It's a picture. Put together, by deliberation. A design. Colour
disposed against mass, tone against line, volume against plane. Look at
it! *It's out there!* Impersonal. Objective. I – am – not – involved!

METTE

Not involved – with Justine's nakedness?

GAUGIN

Not as you think! Naturally, I see her as a man, sensually. But as an
artist, my sensuality sits apart. It is cooled. It has become an aesthetic
quality. That is how it is used. It has been transmuted into thought: a
mode of seeing. It has become a vision. Yes! A woman – naked! But
in a pattern of harmonies that will be forever beautiful and true!

METTE

Just as I thought – sensual and cold – at the same time. That isn't how
she looks to me! She's loose and horrible! Her belly! Look how it
bulges! Her breasts – how they sag!

GAUGUIN

That nude is a triumph! It is Nature naturalized! Whole schools of
painters, whole shoals of issue will spring from it. Its caviars will be
seismic! It's unique!

METTE

But no-one has bought it. No-one has offered a franc! Renoir and Monet refused to display alongside a painting of yours. The Academie will exclude it. It's in bad taste.

GAUGIN

Like me! I know. Crude and insensitive, I am!

METTE

You're not like your crony, Schuffenecker.

GAUGUIN

He's genteel! Middle-class. A known quantity.

METTE

Breadwinner! A devoted companion.

GAUGUIN

The wall of your bourgeois mind. You build it higher every time you mention money. Me, here! You, there! It's the *rentier* versus the craftsman, the creator versus mediocrity. I live for my work; you want money. If pictures made francs, you'd paint, too!... But no-one has a right to the raptures of art, if he runs away from its pains. The artist dares all, and will suffer all.

METTE

Even if he loses all? His family? His wife? His livelihood?

GAUGUIN

My need is for you. And the children. And my art!

METTE

Eh, bien! If only we'd all back off, just blend into the background, eh?

GAUGUIN

But no! *Mais non! Ah, merde! merde!* I am going to play my guitar, and sing with the children.

(Sounds of receding footsteps and a guitar beginning to play in the background.)

GAUGUIN

(Calling & fading)

Emile, Clovis, Aline.

METTE

She will have to go, that trollope! That Justine!

(Guitar gets suddenly louder and emphatic in response. Children laughing. silence. A pause.)

NARRATOR

But that wasn't how it waned?

GAUGUIN

Ah, non! I was weak. I played possum. I pretended to submit – for the sake of peace and quiet. I painted landscapes, all landscapes. Not a limb, not a loin! Not a single nude. At the Impressionist exhibition of eighty-two, Huysmans exclaimed: "He is mad. He has lost his vision, his talent for looking. His palette has shrunk. It is scurfy and drab."

METTE

And had you lost your vision?

GAUGUIN

Not on your life! I'd harnessed myself to domesticity like a dray. I drew its cart over the cobbles of Paris, subdued as a saint.

(Suggestion of stock exchange sounds.)

GAUGUIN

Rue des Fourneaux, A la Bourse; from the Bourse to the Rue des Fourneaux. Day in, day out. I did my bit. I won the bread, just as Mette demanded. Weekends, I gave to my daubs.

(Fade out bourse, bring in a baby crying.)

GAUGUIN

But – at the birth of little Paul, my dignity, my pride, my vanity – whatever! – revolted and vaunted itself.

NARRATOR

You mean?

GAUGUIN

I resigned!

NARRATOR

As winner of the bread?

(Fade out sounds of baby crying.)

GAUGUIN

Exactly! Bertin was horrified. "But the Bourse, the Bourse! You play the market like a master. A virtuoso! The shareholders sing!" he said. "Our profits are melodies!" Ha, ha! Like Huysmans, he thought I'd come unhinged.

NARRATOR

Hadn't you? What of your wife, her brood, your home? Your responsibilities as *paterfamilias*?

GAUGUIN

What about my responsibilities to painting? My intuitions, my insights come to me, like the cries of waifs on the wind, waiting for deliverance. I cannot barricade my doors, become the brunt of genesis. My brain engenders the most intangible of heirs. Nuances of an indescribable delicacy evolve like fugitives, ready to flee at the fall of a leaf. They are the progeny of God. His pigments flow afresh each day in holy lines and consecrated colours, as if my canvases were conduits from His ineluctable springs. The greater the artist, the greater the intelligence he is granted. Who must I deny? God or Mette?

NARRATOR

It is a terrible crucifix. I do not know.

GAUGUIN

If I become the man that Mette demands, I am damned as an artist. If I become the artist my being demands, I am damned as a man. I am damned whatever!... I am tired. I am done. I am ill. Shouldn't I sleep, now?

(Bring the sound of the sea into the background to suggest the hospital ward.)

NARRATOR

One more thing! No wonder Mette moaned and tholed. You had no money. Your motives were incomprehensible. You offered no security, no certainty, no future. How could you expect her to abide and endure?

GAUGUIN

You're right, of course! But my defection wasn't complete. I promised Bertin to help part-time at the Bourse, for one whole year. Which I did. I earned and I yearned. Only then did I break with Bertin. But not with Mette. I was thirty-six years old, the father of five. Yes! And still an apprentice! A Sunday painter! I was desperate. We fought. We argued. And finally, she – eh – deferred. In the Winter of eighty-five. We removed to Rouen, where Pissarro painted: The people, the plazas, the streets, and the great cathedral. Ah! The contemplations of God! Then, Denmark! What a letdown! At Winter's end, exiled in Copenhagen. We stayed with the Gadds. Mette was luminous with gratitude. She had proved her point! I had failed as a painter, as a husband, and as a father. And no money and no job, a miserable pauper, to boot. Oh, the Nordic Gads! Ah, the Nordic gods! They dropped their curses on my dreams. What could I do? I just had to go. Clovis and I departed, bequeathing Denmark to the Danes. I prayed for Winter to usurp the year and, long before the solstice, to ice it over like a Christmas cake. In Paris, it was Summer.

NARRATOR

It is Summer *here*. It's always Summer in Martinique. That is why you came.

(Bring up slightly the sounds of the sea.)

GAUGUIN

It is partly why I came.

NARRATOR

Tell me!

GAUGUIN

I am tired! I am done! I am ill! You've delighted your ear with discords. You've denied my requests. I had no longings to listen to Mette and her recriminations. I wanted to rest and retreat.

VOICE ONE

But listen to the sea! Its susurrus will hasten you.

VOICE FIVE

Its cloth has an edge of lace. Look at it! Are you quickening?

GAUGUIN

I know its shores are dark. They are thirsty for light. It is unfolding a dismal cloth, displaying its sadnessess and deepening its glooms of damsons, plums and burgundies – an infinity of bruises. Its waves are extruding its agonies. There is something on the beach. It is me. I lie like a crucified man. I am cold. The waves are nibbling at my flesh, like the claws of crabs. The sun hasn't sympathy enough to warm my wounds. The prestidigitations of the sea are rolling me below the palms like potter's clay. I am tired. I am ill. It is perfecting me like a sphere.

(Bring up the sea-sounds & mix with the daily sounds of the hospital ward.)

NARRATOR

Once more, his senses flit, bat-winged and blind, out of the darkening shadows of his mind. The day and his honeycombed nerves are emptied and quiet. The corals desist. The wafer of the moon, hauling in its tides and tunes on miraculous strings, transubstantiates its purities into the things of night. We must wait. Perhaps his abstention from light, or absence from longing will heal him? Meanwhile, the odours and sounds of Saint Pierre return to its streets, its courtyards, its houses and shrines. With the stealth of the `Fer-de-lance' of Martinique, the fanging taste of ash from Mont Pelee strikes at the air: Its dacites, limestones, andecites and tuffs are slinking down its flanks like terrorists. Infernos of oranges, limes and lemons flare up: their frenzy is terrifying. They turn inward, and become intense, like illnesses.

(Over a background of sea-sounds in the distance, and the sounds of a tropical night, superimpose snatches of voices, the bedsprings of patients, et cetera. The footsteps of Sister and nurse enter, and visit beds here and there. They arrive at Gauguin's bed.)

NURSE

Our Frenchman seems asleep, Sister. Shall I disturb him?

SISTER

If he is peaceful, no! *Mais, attendez!* Suppose he is sinking again? Has he got a pulse, Nurse?

NURSE

It goes hoppety-skip.

SISTER

Something has arrested him. See to it, Nurse!

NURSE

Oui, ma soeur! Je m'occuperai de lui. Mon pauvre!

(Pattings of bedclothes, sounds of administering, et cetera. After a while, the nurse speaks)

NURSE

C'est ca, c'est ca, mon pauvre! Maintenant,
Vous avez besoin de dormir.

(Fade to silence.)

NARRATOR

Night passes. Another dawn. Another pilgrimage. He is travelling towards himself. He is imminent. But his wholeness will not heed. Two lodestars tug at him. The one says: "Become companion to Mette, your wife!" The other: "Become your art's artificer. And God's." Both are segregated tasks.
Both are therefore damned. His love for Mette has many elements.

(Fade in sounds of guitar, children & domestic sounds.)

NARRATOR

...The gnawing of his conscience, the nexus of habit, a passion for his bairns, a preference for security, and what no third eye can see: the lure of her he's famished for. In that, he does not change; and that is what she spurns. But his love for his art and his God are one. For him, the sanctity of the spirit and the verity of Art are indivisible. Yet, it will entice him into strange and savage paths. *L'etranger en sauvage.* Let us wait. Let us wait. He groans in his sleep. He is groaning at the dawn.

(Sounds of movements in the ward & morning sounds. Then a melange of: sea-sounds, his children, guitar music, mother calling `paul, paul', mette abusing justine, sounds of sailing and laughter. Then fade all but morning hospital sounds held in background.)

NARRATOR

He isn't coming to. He will not come round. He does not want to see, to hear, to smell, to touch and taste the outside world. He's going to ground, slinking again into the burrow of himself, his senses blunt as earth.

VOICE FIVE

Open your eyes and look!

VOICE ONE

Open your ears and hear!

VOICE TWO

To quicken your heart, sniff in the odours on the breeze.

VOICE THREE

Let your fingers feel the sheets they touch.

VOICE FOUR

Drink! Slake your thirst on satisfactions. Let their juices linger.

VOICE TWO

(Interjecting)

They will make your breathing fragrant.

VOICE FOUR

And fill your heart brimful of essences.

NARRATOR

They are trying. They are transmitting their currents and codes. They want him to collaborate, these *confreres* of his consciousness.

VOICE ONE

Try to remember your memories! Remember Manet! Manet!

NARRATOR

We contend, we contend!

GAUGUIN

(Groans)

VOICE FIVE

Come on! Awake! The shore is putting on the sun's integument like a threadbare surplice that shadows have burst.

GAUGUIN

(Faintly)

Tell me!

NARRATOR

They are winning! He's trying to awake.

VOICE ONE

Yes? Tell you what?

GAUGUIN

Tell me about the corn-poppy? Is it bleeding in the fields?
Is its calyx thrown?

NARRATOR

He is back in another land, buried in another time.

GAUGUIN

Is there a white world in the wind and holy words: albino fields,
striated trees, black-cassocked priests? And prayers?

VOICE FIVE

All right! Keep them close, if you must. Watch with your inner eye.
But see!

GAUGUIN

Are there kissing berries. And the tastes of Christmas?

NARRATOR

He is wilful. He will not fuse. He will not awake.

GAUGUIN

Are there chocolates, children, carols and carraway cakes?

NARRATOR

Beside his personal hurt, the pain of his fever fades.

GAUGUIN

Mette, Mette, Oh Mette! Mon Emile, Clovis, Aline – *ma chere Aline*, Jean et Paul. And Manet! What of Manet? Eduourde, Eduourde!

NARRATOR

You know he died. You know! Manet died.

GAUGUIN

I know. It was sudden and easy as a sigh. God gave him the nod, and Manet ceased. It frightened me! Thirty-five, and little had come to fruit. That was the Spring of eighty-three. By the start of eighty-four, we'd removed to Rouen; by the Winter of eighty-four, to icy Copenhagen. I soon de-camped, and Mette concurred. She refused to leave, to accompany me! Mette, Oh Mette! Am – I – not – enough?

NARRATOR

If we're going to save him, he needs the stickiness of happier times. He's distancing himself, again, becoming an amalgam of departures. Like the stars of the universe, he's flying apart.

VOICE FIVE

We'll talk him back.

VOICE ONE

Let us trounce him into oneness!

VOICE 4

I will be our spokesman.

VOICE TWO

You! Why you?

VOICE FOUR

I am the organ of speech, as well as the limb of taste.

VOICE THREE

He's stymied you there! I can't touch that reply. Unless our patient
knows Braille.

VOICE FOUR

He doesn't! It's settled, then. I will proceed.

VOICE ONE

So pompous!

VOICE FOUR

Artists react to ritual, anything ceremonial. Anyway, a little gilt on the
gingerbread sweetens the throat.

VOICE ONE

A loud bang would be much better than pomposity.

VOICE FOUR

I'll ignore your jibes! And apostrophize the patient.

VOICE ONE

Apostrophize the patient!
(Laughs)

VOICE TWO

Proceed! The odour of contention is unpleasant.

VOICE FOUR

Attention! Wake up! We, who are as good as you, swear to you, who
are no better than we—

VOICE ONE

Riddles!

VOICE FOUR

He responds, also, to circumlocutions. It worked for you!

VOICE ONE

(Murmurs) That's true! That's true!

VOICE FOUR

(Continuing)—Swear to you, who are no better than we, that our re-
union is overdue. If you remain intact, we shall all endure; if not, it's
d—d—discontinuance.

(A silence. Only the usual sounds are heard in the ward.)

NARRATOR

What of your boast: Dare all, or dare nothing? What has become of that?

(Silence again.)

NARRATOR

If Manet's name is not the lamp to light him up, perhaps Cezanne's will touch the wick. *Attention! Paul!*
Paul Cezanne!

GAUGUIN

(*Groans & mumbles*) I'm not Cezanne.

NARRATOR

Paul Cezanne!

GAUGUIN

(*More firmly*) I am not Cezanne.

NARRATOR

Who then? Who are you?

GAUGUIN

I am Paul Gauguin.

NARRATOR

And what are you doing, now?

GAUGUIN

Nothing. I am ill, ill!

NARRATOR

Getting better, or worse?

GAUGUIN

What?

NARRATOR

Do you know where you are?

GAUGUIN

Of course!

NARRATOR

And the time?

VOICE FIVE

Morning is filling the corners with colours. Which?

GAUGUIN

How should I know?

VOICE FIVE

Blind?

VOICE FOUR

What is the taste of emptiness?

GAUGUIN

Damn you!

VOICE FOUR

Keep your insolence behind your teeth and sour your thoughts with it!

VOICE FIVE

And glue your eyelids shut!

GAUGUIN

Damn you all! You're goading me! Get back to Paul Cezanne! Didn't he believe in essences? The power behind external things?

NARRATOR

"The essence of a work consists in what is not expressed."

GAUGUIN

That was Mallarme.

NARRATOR

Oh, sorry!

GAUGUIN

Cezanne quoted Mallarme, yes! "The essence is implicit in the arrangement of lines, not materially constituted, without words or colour. The essence of composition is what is NOT expressed."

NARRATOR

Do you defer to that?

GAUGUIN

D'accord! It is exact. I wrote to Schuff about that very point. *C'est ca*! Philosophers tell us often enough. The mystery is veiled. It lies behind the substance of our world. We cannot know direct. But the 'sensation' of the supernatural is what we perceive in things. Objects are symbols. They materialize the Idea! They manifest the mystery!

NARRATOR

That's all very well! Just abstract talk!

GAUGUIN

Abstract talk!

NARRATOR

Those are my sentiments! This `sensation' you talk about! It's easy to claim: We know the 'sensation' of the supernatural. But how do we know? That is the nub of the question.

GAUGUIN

Isn't it obvious?

NARRATOR

Is it?

GAUGUIN

Of course! By means of our senses! How else?

NARRATOR

Exactement! Why spurn your own? *Exactement*!

GAUGUIN

Neat. A clever stratagem! You are trying to trick me into your intentions. Well, it won't work! In any case, Cezanne was a different kettle of fish.

NARRATOR

Different! How?

GAUGUIN

Cezanne had the francs. His pictures sold. I sold little. While my spirit shrivelled with cold in Copenhagen, Cezanne mused away his days in the sun, in the Midi, absorbing Virgil, and analyzing skyscapes from the hills. And so, as his horizons surge aloft, his blues intensify, and his reds are scrums of raucous shouts. His 'sensation' was there! And he was on its scent.

VOICE TWO

Talking of scents—

VOICE ONE

And talking of shouts—

VOICE FIVE

And canvases and colours—

VOICE FOUR

And a thirst for truth—

VOICE THREE

The touch of a brush—

NARRATOR

The sensation of Cezanne! You see! Your senses are part and parcel of yourself. You cannot even think, or recollect, without their help. Deny them, deny yourself!

GAUGUIN

I know.

ALL

He knows!

NARRATOR

We are making progress! Your 'sensation'? Where did you seek it?

GAUGUIN

I did not seek for it at all. It sought for me! Poverty drove me to Pont-Aven. Paris was dear. I was starving. I was ill. I simply wanted to survive. The Celts of Brittany called out. My longings for a sun-baked indolence and intimations of the Primitive. Their plaids, their sabots, their propitiation of a stringent God, seemed primeval: It linked them to the Indians of Peru. The echo of sabots on granite was strong and grand. To Schuff, I said: I'm looking for that sound in my art.

NARRATOR

So your '*sensation*' revealed itself.

GAUGUIN

Yes. Their reverence for essentials awoke in me – Contempt.

NARRATOR

Contempt!

GAUGUIN

For the false. For the coverings, the urban cosmetic of hypocrisy. It awoke in me the savage that I am.

NARRATOR

You – savage?
Only in the head! How can savages survive without the use of five good senses?

GAUGUIN

All right! All right! You've won your point. Let them present their briefs.

VOICE FIVE

Fine! Look! The mountains seem small. They snout like moles, blinded with the bloom of distance, damsoned through clouds, they're dozing in the sun.

GAUGUIN

No! The snows of Brittany are calling me. I need to cool.

VOICE THREE

So, it's comfort you seek?

GAUGUIN

No! I hunger for basics: burnt umber, below, earth; above, white birds, white herons trailing their cerements across the weeping fields. And, my future opening like a wound.

VOICE FIVE

Are you painting a picture of exits and departures?

GAUGUIN

Not at all! It was at Pont-Aven and Le Pouldu, where first the corner
of the veil curled slightly in the wind; when I knew I'd have to suffer
for my art.

NARRATOR:

What day, what mood?

GAUGUIN

Pont-Aven. A turbulent day. The dawn tumescent with wood-smoke,
snow and ice; and the starlings, the sadness of starlings, wheeling,
wheeling. They were as dark as locusts in a drained-out sky. Yes! And
the wrens. Ah! the wrens; small and dim, but unquenchable. I felt like
a wren. It was a time of origins. Something had begun.

VOICE THREE

Was there snow, the fine and feathery kind?

VOICE ONE

No! It rang like shot against the panes.

GAUGUIN

Correct! And sewn in cords of white the furrows were; with
threadbare fields, hemmed in ochres round their selvages.

VOICE FIVE

And winter wheat, a petit-point in green.

VOICE FOUR

On balance, I prefer to call it castor sugar, scattered by a thrifty cook.

VOICE TWO

A gourmet's needs! For me, the crispness of the wind! That scalpelled smell, astringent, salient as desire! That stays! That stays!

GAUGUIN

All of you were there. But – I might have guessed you'd garble things. The way they tell it, the essences of things are lost! They all forget the heave and weight of the sky, waiting to fall, when the world tilts. One day, the world will tilt on me. Mette has put her finger to it. It inclines! It inclines!

NARRATOR

Let nothing dismay you, now! You are gathering to a fullness.

GAUGUIN

I know it. But, at their best, our senses are merely keys to a walled and sinful garden. They open doors to abundancies of Eves, and our incompetent Edens.

NARRATOR

Ah, just so! Those Eves and the sweetness of their apples! Mette believed you had bitten into many cores, even the model you used for your '*Etude du Nu*'.

GAUGUIN

Justine! I remember her with joy. Such roominess! Such accommodation! Her bounty won't be seen again until the last hiatus comes.

NARRATOR

So Mette was right! Her juice was running on your tongue!

GAUGUIN

Wrong! As artist, I am freed from action. Desire and act combine in art. I act through paint. Still, I will admit, as man, I wanted her. Between her vegetative thighs, my maleness grew like a metaphor, crisp and dark. But that was all!

NARRATOR

Commendable!

GAUGUIN

Her kettle was furred.

NARRATOR

So your virtue was forced! Funny! Very funny!

GAUGUIN

Do you know what the peasants of Brittany say?

NARRATOR

Should I? Tell me, but make it brief.

GAUGUIN

"A standing phallus has no conscience." Cunning or prudence? So what of Paul Gauguin, the Borgia from Peru, no more a man than most. And no less.

NARRATOR

Maybe. But more of an artist than most.

GAUGUIN

So tell me of a greater grief. It will lessen mine.

NARRATOR

Submerge your griefs in the joy of your art.

GAUGUIN

Easier said than done. Even now, a grey disturbance spreads across my mind and over the estuary of the Loire. The solitary whiteness of a swan is seeking, seeking for a patch of blue to rock and rest in.

NARRATOR

Return to the here and now! The present will free you from what is past. Perhaps you've noticed? We've heard nothing from the sensual five, for some while, now?

GAUGUIN

Something is brewing.

NARRATOR

Taking their places is all.

GAUGUIN

Not before time.

NARRATOR

They need to settle. Who is chief?

GAUGUIN

I thought it was clear.

NARRATOR

Not so to them.

VOICE ONE

Certainly not!

VOICE THREE

That's right!

VOICE FOUR

Exactement!

VOICE TWO & VOICE FIVE

(Together) D'accord! D'accord!

GAUGUIN

At least, they know the artist isn't born in one whole piece. Those who condemn are ignorant of all that is in his nature. Mette imprisoned herself, and me, in terms like *'pere'* and *'mere'*: Concepts, Conventions and Roles! *They* know the struggle to stay brimful and intact!

VOICE ONE

We do! But where do we stand, the one to the other? Which of us is prime? For instance, you play *and* sing.

GAUGUIN

The piano badly.

VOICE ONE

But the guitar well.

(A few notes are struck on the guitar.)

GAUGUIN

True, true!

VOICE ONE

And Beethoven you revere.

(A few bars of Beethoven's 'pathetique' piano sonata are heard.)

VOICE ONE

He reverberates in your head. True? You know his techniques. You ponder them. His harsh oriental chants, opposed by vibrant notes in a nearby key: the rich accompaniment. These words are yours, not so?

GAUGUIN

Agreed! But that was analogy alone. To enable me to commit to canvas, a musical sense of colour, a repetition of tones in a true Beethovenian sequence!

VOICE ONE

But if you were deaf, how to define it at all? Unable to hear, he knew the agonies that ensued. Cut off, enclosed in himself, he lost his marvellous harmonies. Deafness severed him – from music, and from people.

VOICE FIVE

But blindness separates us all from every thing.

VOICE TWO

A world without scents is one from which the poignancy of the past,
and the astonishment of the actual, have flown away.

VOICE THREE

Sans moi, the texture of loving is lost!

VOICE FOUR

What about the spite of thirst, the savour of salt, and the indefinable
hunger for the wafer of Christ.

NARRATOR

They plead like plaintiffs in the dock.

GAUGUIN

They are not on trial. I need them all. How to paint if I haven't sensed
their colours first? In Martinique, old leaves fall without suggesting
sounds. It's more like the touch of spirits from the dark. How, without
their help, to put it down? Their affidavits sworn, I'm free to paint the
whichness and whateverness of everything there is.

*(The sounds of children come up out of the past; and the voice of
Mette.)*

METTE

Venez, venez, mes enfants. Supper time!

ALINE

Papa! ou est papa, maman?

PAUL

Papa!

(The sounds from the past recede.)

NARRATOR

Are you artist enough to distil their essences, too?

GAUGUIN

Suffering brings a poetry of its own. I must endure it all for art. Of all the arts, painting is the most sublime. Like music, it reaches through the senses to the soul. The ear grasps one note at a time; whereas, the eye takes in everything at once; and, as it sees, it simplifies.

VOICE FIVE

I've won!

VOICE ONE

Just wait! He hasn't finished yet.

GAUGUIN

Words and paint say what they want to say. But only painting says it all at once. Reading and music require the will to hear. Sight alone compels an instantaneous response. You're at the beck and call of the writer's mind when you read. Looking at pictures, listening to music, you're free to dream the dreams that strengthen and sustain.

VOICE TWO

But odours free you most of all!

GAUGUIN

You are right! But odours are transient. They cannot be composed.
And if they could, it would only be a trivial art.

VOICE THREE

What of touch?

VOICE FOUR

Or taste?

GAUGUIN

Smell, taste and touch, important as they are, are subalterns. The eye
is Commander-in-Chief. C.O! The eye remembers; the ear forgets. So
do the rest.

ALL

(General protest from the 4 senses.)

VOICE FIVE

Silence! Attention! This is your C.O. speaking.

GAUGIN

In a manner of speaking, only! From now on, – nothing! You are bound by an order of silence. All bulletins, all intelligences, come through me. Are you clear? You are informers, only.

(Expand and contract the last question to suggest he is coming to consciousness at last, over sound of footsteps entering the ward.)

GAUGUIN

Comprenez-vous?

NURSE

What must I understand, Monsieur?

GAUGUIN

(Silence)

NURSE:

Rien, eh? Do not fret, monsieur. A dream. *Seulement, un reve.*

(Sound of footsteps going away. A suggestion of the sea in the background.)

NARRATOR

He is coming together. Listen! His sea-corals build and their colours have broken through. They are luminous, like cells in a brain. His senses flicker, out and in like fish, but stay submerged, getting to know their habitats, and the silence of their own terrains. Soon, Gauguin, soon, you must awake!

GAGUIN

I'm almosting it. I am readying myself – to see as meant . To see: sun
and moon, stained globes, ragged spheres, perils of flesh, thrust of
petal, push of leaf, of breast, of thigh, and all the harmonies of things,
as God created them. I'll paint His pure Ideas; infuse materials with
His messages. Meanwhile, I'll live the savage life, as free and prodigal
as a pawpaw seed!

NARRATOR

They'll call you libertine, lustful, selfish – as your wife has done.

GAUGUIN

Thus – my canvases will admit the 'me' they think is me. But,
penetrating eyes will pierce the paint and find the living me beneath. If
I am to throw new lineaments onto space, extend our seeing to the
limits of sight, vibrate the strings and the colours of God, I must put on
the disguise of my own imperfect idioms.

NARRATOR

Won't that be deceit?

GAUGUIN

Art is unavoidable deceit: a symbol, a mask. But a mask that reveals.
Just think! Disguised by word, but nakedly true, I can feel the savage
dancing in my heart! The leap of the jubilant child, the lilt of the
blood, the tongue attempting its meanings. All – I shall commit them
all to canvas and paint, to ink and to clay.

NARRATOR

At last he is whole! At last he is healed!

(Suggest in sound, as he speaks, that the patient has left the inside of his head & he is now back in the ward, fully conscious. The bedsprings creak as He begins to sit up, climbs upright on the bed, and stands there. As he is doing so, footsteps are entering the ward.)

GAUGUIN

(Calling) Aline! Aline!

NURSE

Sister, Sister! *Vite, vite!*
Monsieur Gauguin is climbing on his bed.

GAUGUIN

Aline! Aline!

(Another pair of footsteps hurry in.)

SISTER

What is it, Nurse? *Oh, mon Dieu*!
He will injure himself. He must be stopped.

GAUGUIN

Aline!

NURSE

He is calling for his daughter. Shall I get help?

SISTER

No, wait! He is going to speak again. Listen!

GAUGUIN

Aline! Ma petite, ma petite fleur!

NURSE

Is he hallucinating?

SISTER

I do not think so. Let us wait!

GAUGUIN

You, Aline, of all my children, will understand my words. Perhaps you can help your mother to understand, also?

SISTER

Is he going to pray? He is making the sign of the cross! A strange stance for a prayer!

NURSE

It is, Sister! Now, he's holding up his palms, as if he's going to—

(Fading out as soon as Gauguin begins to speak.)

(Perhaps the following speech can be foregrounded in some way? The words are translated from one of Guaugin's own letters.)

GAUGUIN

I believe that the sanctity of the spirit and the truth of art are one and indivisible. I believe that art issues from a Holy Spring, and lives in the heart of every man that acknowledges His celestial light. I believe that after one has tasted the sublime flavours of great art, one is fatally and forever bound to it. I believe that, by its intervention, every living man can arrive at his own beatitude. I believe in a last judgment; that all those who dare to trade and profit by art, which is chaste and sublime; all those who have soiled and degraded it by the baseness of their sentiments, by their materialism and vile covetousness, will be condemned to terrible ends. And, finally, I believe that the disciples who have remained faithful to their art will be glorified, will be folded in melodious cloths of harmony, and will be returned to the Divine Spring from whence they came; and they will bathe forever in its flowing memories.

SISTER

Nurse, this is a special man. He frightens me. What he has said is both a beautiful prayer and a terrible curse.

NURSE

Perhaps it would have been best if we'd let him die.

SISTER

Don't dare to think such a thing! *Alors!* Let us leave him alone. He is over the fever, now. And this is not the time to try to plump his pillows and straighten his bed. We can attend to him, later. Let us go, nurse!

(Footsteps withdraw. Fade in guitar music & children laughing and playing. Hold behind the final speech.)

NARRATOR

And so Paul Gauguin awoke! Awakened to health, and awoke to himself. His separation from Mette, his wife, and his five children, had almost broken him. I, and my five friends, have served our turn. And now, all that anyone can do is to leave him to himself, and let him pursue his savage pilgrimage to wherever it will lead him.

(End on the sounds of the breakers of a tropical sea and creoles singing, as the play began)

About the Author

Roy Holland was born in Birmingham. He went to Africa in 1966 to teach in the universities of the Boleswa countries. In 1971 he went to Greece for three years. He and his family lived on the island of Levkas for six months, the Gulf of Corinth for a similar period, and in Corfu for a little over two years. He wrote full-time until 1974, when he returned to the U.K. and worked on a research project until returning to Africa in 1977. Thereafter he lived in Southern Africa and worked in universities in Zimbabwe, Lebowa and Venda. He was Professor of English at the University of the North, the University of Venda, as well as Dean of the Faculty of Arts in the later 80's. He retired early to write full-time, and now lives in Ledbury, Herefordshire.

www.ingramcontent.com/pod-product-compliance
Lightning Source LLC
Chambersburg PA
CBHW031114260626
47172CB00001B/371